Martin Luther King Jr. Day

For Jayden Smith
—M. M.

ALADDIN PAPERBACKS
An imprint of Simon & Schuster Children's Publishing Division
1230 Avenue of the Americas, New York, NY 10020
Text copyright © 2007 by Brenda Bowen
Illustrations copyright © 2007 by Mike Gordon
All rights reserved, including the right of reproduction
in whole or in part in any form.
READY-TO-READ, ALADDIN PAPERBACKS, and related logo
are registered trademarks of Simon & Schuster, Inc.
Also available in an Aladdin Library edition.
Designed by Sammy Yuen Jr.
The text of this book was set in Century Schoolbook BT.
Manufactured in the United States of America
First Aladdin Paperbacks edition December 2007
2 4 6 8 10 9 7 5 3 1
Library of Congress Cataloging-in-Publication Data
McNamara, Margaret.
Martin Luther King, Jr. Day / by Margaret McNamara ; illustrated by
Mike Gordon.—1st Aladdin Paperbacks ed.
p. cm.—(Robin Hill School) (Ready-to-read)
Summary: Mrs. Connor's students at Robin Hill School share their
dreams for the future after learning about the day that celebrates the
life and dream of Dr. Martin Luther King, Jr.
ISBN-13: 978-1-4169-3494-3 (pbk.)
ISBN-10: 1-4169-3494-4 (pbk.)
ISBN-13: 978-1-4169-3495-0 (lib. bdg.)
ISBN-10: 1-4169-3495-2 (lib. bdg.)
1. Martin Luther King, Jr., Day—Juvenile fiction.
[1. Martin Luther King, Jr., Day—Fiction. 2. Conduct of life—Fiction.
3. Schools—Fiction.] I. Gordon, Mike, ill. II. Title.
PZ7.M232518Mar 2007
[E]—dc22
2007019003

Robin Hill School

Martin Luther King Jr. Day

WITHDRAWN

Written by Margaret McNamara
Illustrated by Mike Gordon

Ready-to-Read
Aladdin Paperbacks
New York   London   Toronto   Sydney

One day in January, Mrs. Connor took the first graders to a museum.

"Does anyone know
who this is?" she asked.

Ayanna knew the answer.
"That is the Reverend Doctor
Martin Luther King Junior,"
said Ayanna.

Mrs. Connor said,
"Doctor King was a
great leader because he
had great dreams."

"What kind of dreams?"
asked Reza.

"They were very big dreams,"
said Mrs. Connor,
"about how to make the
world a better place."

Back at school, Mrs. Connor asked the class to draw their dreams on a piece of paper.

They had big dreams,
just like Doctor King.

"I have a dream that there
will be no more fighting,"
Eigen said.

13

"I have a dream that the earth will be clean," said Hannah.

"I have a dream that
everyone will have fun,"
Katie said.

"I have a dream that people
will never get sick!"
Nia said.

19

"I have a dream that I will do good things," said Becky.

"I have a dream that all children will play together," Emma said.

"I have a dream that no one will be poor," said James.

"I have a dream that everyone will be safe," Reza said.

The first graders were happy
with their dreams.

"Doctor King would be proud
of you," said Mrs. Connor.

"What is your dream?"
Ayanna asked Mrs. Connor.

"Oh, I have a very big dream," said Mrs. Connor.

"I have a dream,"
said Mrs. Connor,
"that all your dreams
will come true."